Disney · PIXAR

Cars 3

W9-CAV-363

Thunder Hollow Crazy Eight Racers!

By Kristen L. Depken
Illustrated by the Disney Storybook Art Team

A Random House PICTUREBACK® Book
Random House 🏠 New York

Materials and characters from the movie *Cars 3*. Copyright © 2017 Disney Enterprises, Inc. and Pixar. All rights reserved.
Published in the United States by Random House Children's Books, a division of Penguin Random House LLC,
1745 Broadway, New York, NY 10019, and in Canada by Penguin Random House Canada Limited, Toronto. Pictureback,
Random House, and the Random House colophon are registered trademarks of Penguin Random House LLC.
randomhousekids.com
ISBN 978-0-7364-3728-8
Printed in the United States of America
10 9 8 7 6 5 4 3 2 1

Welcome to Thunder Hollow Speedway, home of the Crazy Eight demolition derby!

Each and every week, daring cars of all shapes and sizes try to crash and smash their way to becoming champion of the Thunder Hollow Crazy Eight. Let's meet some of the wild and wacky racers!

Miss Fritter, a rough-and-tumble school bus, is the undefeated Crazy Eight champion. Watch out when she's on the track—the Diva of Demolition stops for no one!

I'm about to commit a moving violation!

Yahoo!

Arvy is an old recreational vehicle with a big sense of humor and an even bigger drive to win. He's ready to send the other racers on a permanent vacation!

Woop woop! Move over or get run over!

Dr. Damage is an ambulance who loves to enter the race with his sirens blaring. When you hear them, move out of the way—fast!

The Thunder Hollow Speedway is a quarter-mile dirt track in the shape of a figure eight—and it's about to be taken over by these fearless racers!

Today there are two newcomers on the track: Chester Whipplefilter and Frances Beltline. The other racers would be shocked to learn that these contestants are actually Lightning McQueen and Cruz Ramirez in disguise! Lightning and Cruz have no idea what they've gotten themselves into. . . .

Miss Fritter revs her engine and heads straight for Cruz. Luckily, Lightning pushes her out of the way in the nick of time. Miss Fritter circles around and tries to crush Lightning instead. Thinking quickly, Lightning shoves a pile of tires into her path, which sends the rowdy school bus crashing through her own billboard!

Several cars continue to smash and bash their way around the track until finally, Cruz is the last one standing. She is the winner of the Crazy Eight demolition derby!

Cruz is so excited, she bumps into Mr. Drippy, the water truck.

As he falls on his side, water splashes everywhere, washing off Lightning's muddy disguise.

"It's Lightning McQueen!" the fans cheer.

Lightning and Cruz hurry away. But they'll always remember their amazing night at the Thunder Hollow Crazy Eight demolition derby!

Temporary Tattoo Directions

1. Cut out tattoo.
2. Peel off protective layer from the tattoo sheet.
3. Put tattoo facedown against skin; press firmly.
4. Wet back of tattoo with damp cloth or sponge.
5. Wait 30 seconds, slide off paper backing, and wipe off tattoo lightly with a wet towel.

To remove, wipe gently with household rubbing alcohol or baby oil under parental supervision.

NOTE: Do not apply to sensitive skin or near eyes.

Ingredients: Acrylates/VA Copolymer, Castor Oil, Ethyl Cellulose, TC0011 Black, TC0023 White, TC0025 Yellow, TC0018 Red, TC002 Blue

Safety Tested and Nontoxic

Manufactured in the United States of America

s, Inc. and Pixar Animation Studios. All rights reserved.

EREVER BOOKS ARE SOLD.

Disney · PIXAR

Cars 3

Over **30** Tattoos!

SCHOOL BUS

Park

Random House
randomhousekids.com

A Random House
PICTUREBACK® Book

US $4.99 / $6.99 CAN
ISBN 978-0-7364-3728-8
50499

9 780736 437288